George Cadenhead

The Family of Cadenhead

George Cadenhead

The Family of Cadenhead

ISBN/EAN: 9783337379957

Printed in Europe, USA, Canada, Australia, Japan

Cover: Foto ©Andreas Hilbeck / pixelio.de

More available books at **www.hansebooks.com**

THE

FAMILY OF CADENHEAD

BY

GEORGE CADENHEAD

ADVOCATE IN ABERDEEN

ABERDEEN

J. & J. P. EDMOND & SPARK

1887

CONTENTS.

A

vi.   *Contents.*

INTRODUCTION.

CADENHEAD, like a great many other lowland Scottish surnames, seems to have had a territorial origin, and it is in Ettrick Forest, in Selkirkshire, that the locality is found from which it had been adopted. The Forest, as it was commonly called, was a Royal domain as far back as distinct history reaches. Its divisions were called Forest-steads, and were occupied, subject to the Royal rights, by tenants, for agriculture and pasturage, at rents payable partly in money and partly in cattle. These occupiers were called kindly tenants, and they seem to have enjoyed fixity of tenure. The Forest itself, and sometimes single steads or groups of steads, were often granted by the Crown to individuals, but this did not disturb the kindly tenants in their holdings. The donatories of the Crown only enjoyed the right to collect the rents. In the 12th century King David I. conferred the Forest on the Abbot of Kelso. Early in the 14th century it was granted to Sir William Douglas, nephew of the good Sir James. In 1403 King Henry IV. conferred it on Earl Percy. In the middle of the 15th century King James II. granted it to William, Earl of Douglas, and five years afterwards, on the forfeiture of the Douglases, it was annexed to the Crown by Act of Parliament. In 1488 it was again conferred on the Angus branch of the Douglas family, the King remaining Fiar. After this the Forest was harried and desolated by the border thieves till James V., by vigorous measures, reduced them to order, when it is recorded that the King's sheep, 10,000 in number, had leave to pasture in quietness.

In 1587 the Forest was feudalised, and the families which had possessed as kindly tenants had feu-charters given to them. At this time the family of Pringle got large feu-grants in the Forest. The Pringles seem to have been of the stock of ancient Britons. Their name was, in ancient times, Hop-Pringle, which is supposed to have been still more anciently O' Pringill or Ap Pringill.

There were two ancient families of Pringle, whose connection, though uncertain, was taken for granted. One was of Torsonce, and their lands lay chiefly on the upper parts of Galla Water and the adjoining portions of Berwickshire and East Lothian.

The other division of the family was called of Whitsun, and later of Smailholm, and sometimes of Galashiels. Of this branch were the families of Tynnis or Buckholm, Trinlyknow, Craiglatch, Torwoodlee, Blyndlee, and Woodhouse or Whytbank; and also some on the Cheviot border, Clifton, Hownam, Sharpitlaw, &c. The lands of this branch lay chiefly on the lower parts of the Gala and on the Cadon Water.

Robert Hop Pringill of Whitsun, to whom the Earl of Douglas gave a charter addressed "dilecto suo scutifero," was afterwards armour bearer and squire of the body to James, Earl of Douglas, at the battle of Otterburn, and held the same post to Archibald, the fourth Earl, afterwards Duke of Turenne, whom he accompanied when sent to France with 10,000 auxiliaries to the assistance of Charles VII., and lost his life, along with his master, at the battle of Verneuil, on 17th August, 1424.

The grandson of this Robert Hop Pringill was James Pringle of Smailholm, who married Isabella Murray, of the family of Falahill, and from his son, William, descended the family of Pringle of Torwoodlee, who are still possessors of that property, and of all or most of the Forest-steads upon the Cadon Water, and amongst these the property now called Cadonhead.

Several Hop Pringills of Whitsun are found before the time of Robert, the Esquire to the Earl of Douglas, viz., Robert, in the time of Alexander III.; Roger, his son, in the time of King Robert Bruce; Thomas, Roger's son, in the time of King David II.; and Thomas and Adam, sons of the last mentioned Thomas, in 1363.

In 1367 Adam Pringill of Whitsun had a charter of the lands of Knoc and Gilliston, in the barony of Strathauchin in Kincardineshire. He was a member of the Royal General Council, and of the Committee of Dooms. He was laird of Baudifash in Aberdeenshire, and of Long-forgund in Perthshire. He was also a burgess of Aberdeen, and one of the crofts of that burgh bears his name, viz., "Adie Pingle's Croft"; the Scottish familiar rendering of Adam being

"Adie," and "Pingle" being the northern mode of writing the name Pringle.

Soon after the time of this Adam Pringle, the family surname Cadenhead appears, William de Caldanhed, a monk of Newbattle Abbey, being the first person found bearing it. This man is first introduced as being, in 1467, a high official in that Abbey, viz., Cellerarius, that is its factor and treasurer, so that he was probably then in the prime of life, and may have been born about 1420. If he inherited the name, his father would, according to genealogical probability, have been born about 1390. It is not known if the name was adopted then, or somewhat earlier, but there are a number of considerations which establish the probability that it originated in the relationship or identity of its first bearers with the occupiers of the Foreststead in Ettrick of the same name.

The small stream now called Cadon Water rises between two high hills, Windlestrae Law and Deaf Heights, at the contact of the shires of Selkirk, Edinburgh, and Peebles, and, after a south-easterly course of about ten miles, joins the Tweed at Cadonlee, nearly opposite Yair. In the old Exchequer Rolls Cadonhead and

Cadonlee are written Caldanehede and Caldanlee, and though the name of the stream does not occur in these records, it cannot be doubted that in like manner it had been called the Caldon or Caldane. It will be observed in the subsequent notices of the earlier families of Cadenhead that their name was written like that of the Forest-stead, and its usual pronunciation is ascertained by the fact that the monk of Newbattle is in some documents Caldanhed, and in others Cawdinhed.

For six miles or thereby, in its upper course, the Cadon runs through a deep valley, wide enough to have afforded accommodation for many cattle and inhabitants, but so surrounded by steep and high hills, with narrow accesses at various points, that it must have been an important fastness in ancient times, before castles were built in Scotland. In later, but now forgotten times, Windydoors, probably a Royal castle, had been built on the slope of one of these hills, and its ruins still remain, testifying to the excellence of the masonry of its builders.

As to the origin of the name Cadon or Caldon, gaelic scholars suggest that it may have been taken from *coille*, a wood, and *dun*, a hill. The neighbouring hills are now certainly not wooded, but it is supposed that once they were well wooded. In "Historia Nennii, cap. lxiv., De Arturo ; de bellis ejus, anno 488," the seventh battle fought by King Arthur is thus referred to—"septimum bellum fuit in silva Calidonis, id est, Cat coit Celidon." The Caledonian forest is a vague reference, but the words "Cat coit Celidon" indicate that the battle was fought at the junction of two streams, whereof one was the Celidon ; and the resemblance of the Celidon to the Caldon is too striking to be called fanciful. Only one small stream, coming out of Glentanner, joins the Cadon at Blackhow, but the ground there seems too narrow for a great battle, so that if the Celidon is the Cadon, the field of the alleged battle must have been lower down, where Tweed receives the Cadon, that is on Cadonlee.

When Cadonhead was feudalised, the yearly return stipulated for was £50, but the older rents were partly in money and partly in produce. They are thus entered in the Exchequer Rolls—"v^{ti}, j bowkow, j fog mart, 1 full mart de firmis loci de Caldanehede, et xiii^s iiii^d de firmis unius bonelesew in Caldanehede." The writer cannot explain what a "bowkow" is, and can only guess that a "fog mart" is a fat ox. As for a "bonelesew," it is also found written "bondlesure" and "boyndlesew" in the Exchequer Rolls, and the writer cannot explain it farther than that the last two syllables suggest the old English word "lea-sow," which means pasture grass-land.

Newbattle Abbey was in the County of Midlothian, not many miles from the source of the Gala. It belonged to the Benedictines, a wealthy and exclusive order, into which young men only of the best families were admitted ; and, according to the etiquette of the period, Dominus Willelmus Caldanhed must have been a man of consideration to be admitted as a witness to a Royal Charter along with the Earl of Argyle and other witnesses named along with them.

The next time that the name is found is in 1494, when Willelmus Cauldenhed witnesses a charter at Banff, and the association of his name with the other witnesses also indicates him to have been a person of consideration, his designation "scutifer" denoting a rank second to that of a knight and superior to that of a "generosus," or gentleman, and favours the theory that he was closely connected with the family of Pringle. At that date the family of Whitsun was represented by James Pringle of Smailholm, whose wife was Isabella Murray of Falahill, sister to the wife of the Earl of Buchan, the granter of the charter. The Earl was Warden of the Marches, which included Selkirk and Roxburghshires, and it seems probable that William Cauldenhed was an Esquire in his suite. The Bishop of Moray, who also witnesses the charter, was a brother of the Earl of Buchan.

The next occurrences of the name are in Margaret Caldenheid, the deceased spouse of Gilbert Rait, in 1576, and Magnus Caldenheid in Pitteyot, who died in 1613, and the crowd of names in the next two or three generations, all in one district of Kincardineshire and in the neighbourhood of the barony and parish of Strathauchin or Strachan, suggest the possibility that, contemporary with William in Banff, a colony of Cadenheads had settled on the lands acquired by Adam Pringle in the preceding century. Parish and Commissary Registers, however, do not reach so far back, and no ancient land titles are to be found connecting Adam Pringle with the more recent proprietors of the land.

As a Christian name, "Magnus" was extremely rare in Scotland, being almost peculiar to Orkney, and its frequent occurrence in this family and its connections may have arisen from some marriage relation with the family of Mowat, of which there were several substantial branches in the sixteenth and seventeenth centuries in the same district, viz., in Barras, in Redclock, and in Elsick. The chiefs of that family were great proprietors in Orkney, Aberdeenshire and Kincardineshire, and "Magnus" was one of their favourite Christian names. Margaret Cadonheid in Mill of Monqueich (1675) seems to have been at least twice married, and her eldest son's name was George Mowat; but there had probably been an earlier connection to account for Magnus Cadenheid in Pitteyot (1610) bearing that name.

The second husband of Margaret in Mill of Monqueich, by whom she had two sons, Magnus and John Millne, may have been one of the eighteen sons of the Rev. Andrew Milne, who was Minister of Fetteresso for thirty-five years from 1605, and whose wife, on her tombstone, is described as " FÆMINA GENEROSA KATHARINA ÆRESKINA," which signifies that she was a lady of gentle birth.

Janet Cadonheid, who was possessor of Drum-oak in 1655, and who was first Mrs. Robert Bannerman and afterwards Mrs. Robert Burnett, may have been the Janet in Findown to whom Magnus in Pitteyot owed some money, and, considering her position and the pecuniary relations between Magnus in Pitteyot and Alexander Bannerman of Elsick, it is not unlikely that her first husband was a cadet of the family of Elsick, and her second a cadet of the family of Leys.

The exact relationship of Alexander Cadden-heid in Wastertoune of Pitfoddels (1695) to the older families is not known, but the fact that his apparent father-in-law was named Magnus Knolls suggests that he was of the family which seems to have spread from Pitteyot to Drumoak. That Alexander in Wastertoune was the father of Alexander in Stengavel, seems highly probable, and the subsequent descents are certain, viz.: (1) Alexander in Stengavel, (2) Alexander in Westfield, (3) John in Aberdeen, (4) Alexander, Advocate in Aberdeen.

On page 1 of this book the birthday of John, eldest son of Alexander Cadenhead and Jane Shirrefs, is inaccurately stated. The correct date is 23rd February, 1820.

In the following tables, page 22, it was omitted to be mentioned that of Alexander Cadenhead's sisters and brother the first Anne died in childhood, the second Anne, and Barbara, died unmarried, and that John, who was an Advocate in Aberdeen and for many years with his brother joint-Procurator-Fiscal of the City, died unmarried in 1867.

Since the following sheets were printed, Mr. A. D. Fordyce of Fergus, Canada, has kindly looked them over and suggested the undernoted corrections and observations :—

At page 21 Mrs. Benjamin Reid's tradition makes Alexander in Stengavel, married in 1717, and John in Upper Cantley, married in 1773, first cousins; whereas the difference in their ages, amounting probably to fifty years, makes a remoter degree of relationship more probable.

At page 28 the sign "*s.p.*," referring to Anne Morison's first marriage, should be deleted.

At same page the words "and had issue," referring to Katharine Morison's marriage, are to be deleted.

In the table following page 44—under the second line at the fourth name, " Elizabeth "— for *Kinaldie* read *Kinaber.*

In the same table, under the fourth line, read *Jean* instead of *Janet* as the name of Thomas Reid's wife. They were the grand-parents of Dr. Thomas Reid, the eminent Metaphysician. Mrs. David Shirrefs (Jane Lunan) and the Metaphysician seem to have been cousins, their grand-parents having been brother and sister.

SKETCH MAP OF LOCALITIES

GENEALOGIES

OF

ALEXANDER CADENHEAD AND JANE SHIRREFS.

"ON the ninth day of August, one thousand eight hundred and seventeen years, by the Reverend Dr. James Shirrefs, late Senior Minister of Aberdeen, were lawfully married in the house of Robert Burnett, Esquire, No. 11 Nelson Street, Edinburgh, ALEXANDER CADENHEAD, Esquire, Advocate, Aberdeen, and Miss JANE SHIRREFS, daughter of the said Dr. James Shirrefs of Friendville, in the Parish of Old Machar, in presence of the said Robert Burnett and William Gardener, Esquire, Writer to the Signet, Edinburgh." *Parish Register of St. Nicholas.*

The issue of this marriage were :—

    I. Amelia, b. 12 June, 1818 ; d. 10 May, 1852.

    II. John, b. 22 Feb., 1820.

    III. James Shirrefs, b. 30 Nov., 1821 ; d. 22 March, 1863.

    IV. Alexander Shirrefs, b. 3 July, 1823 ; d. 22 May, 1883.

B

V. Brebner, b. 26 Dec., 1824 ; d. 7 Sept., 1877.

VI. George, b. 3 March, 1827.

VII. Anne, b. 14 Dec., 1829.

VIII. David, b. 10 June, 1831 ; d. 11 Jan., 1832.

For the further descents of this family see the Appendix.

XV. CENTURY.

1467
to
1482

On 7th July, 1467, in an Instrument of Resignation and Redonation of certain lands belonging to Newbattle Abbey, taken in presence of King James III. at Perth, the act bears to have been witnessed—"Colino Comite de Argill, Dno. Campbell, Roberto Dno. Boyde, Magro. Jacobo Lyndissay, Jacobo Schaw de Sauquhay, Willmo. Turing et *Dno. Willmo. de Caldanhed* Monacho"; and, in the Instrument of Sasine following, the last-named witness is designed as "Sellerarius Monasterii de Newbottyll," and procurator and attorney for the Abbot. In a number of Instruments, down to 1482, the same man's name occurs sometimes "Cawdinhed," invariably styled "Dominus," while the other monks of the Conventus are simply designated by their names.

1494

On 7th March, 1494, James Stewart, Earl of Buchan (Hearty James), brother uterine of James II., and warden of the East Marches, and a brother-in-law of

Pringle of Whitsun, in whose possession the " Stead "
of Ettrick Forest, called Caldonheid, was, and in
whose family it is said to have been time beyond record,
signed a Charter at Banff, " Coram reuerendo in
" Christo patre Andrea Episcopo Moraviensi honora-
" bilibus et famosis viris Patricio Stewart de Latheris
" Johanne Gordon de Lunger *Willelmo Cauldenhed*
" Quintino Shewill et Johanne Willelmi *Scutiferis,*
" Dominis Alexandro Johnstoune et Johanne Gilgour
" presbiteris, cum diversis aliis." The Earl of Buchan
and the Bishop were full brothers. Stewart of Laithers
was akin to the Royal House, and Gordon of Lunger
(Lumgair) was the male representative of the House
of Gordon. The title " Scutifer " inferred a rank
between a Gentleman and a Knight.

Here may fitly be mentioned a tradition, recorded
as follows :—" I, Margaret Cadenhead or Reid, being
" now in my eighty-third year, testify that my Father,
" who was born in 1750, told me that when he was a
" boy, a Dr. Dalrymple had informed him, that two
" brothers of the name of Cadenhead, had come from
" the South, from a place called Caddon water ; that
" one of them had gone to Buchan, and that the other
" had settled on Deeside ; that we had descended
" from the latter." And it is to be noted that in the
old divisions of Scotland, Banff was the capital city of

the district of Buchan. Mrs. Reid was a daughter of William Cadenhead and Margaret Duncan. See Old Machar, 1782.

XVI. CENTURY.

1502   Alexander, Earl of Buchan, son and heir of the deceased Earl James, had a lawsuit with *Willsam Caldanhede* and Alexander Robertson, burgesses of Banff.

1505   In an Inquisition held on the Castlehill of Banff on 11th February, 1505, by Sir Walter Ogilvie of Boyne, Sheriff of the County, to serve Margaret Hepburn, heiress to her brother, Alexander Hepburn of Gargunnock, the first on the Jury was "Andreas Dun de Raty," and the second was " *Willelmus Caldenheid.*" In those days the law was that "Brieves of Inqueists suld be served in plaine Court be the maist worthy of the Schireffdome."

No other old trace of the surname has been found in any part of Scotland beyond the Counties of Kincardine and Aberdeen.

1576   The Estate of *Margaret Caldenheid*, spouse to Gilbert Rait, in Cowtown in Fetteresso, next parish to Strachan, is found recorded in the Register of the Commissariot of Edinburgh, by her two sons George and James. She died on 14th September, 1576, and presumably had not been born later than 1530, perhaps earlier, and possibly in the end of the fifteenth century. Her estate amounted to £388 14s. Scots. She had "twentie drawand oxin," and a good store of "ky," "calfis," "beistis" and "scheip," besides "thrie hors." In the house she had four bolls of meal and four bolls of malt. Commissariot of Edinburgh. Testaments, Vol. 5.

XVII. XVIII. & XIX. CENTURIES.

1610   In this year *Magnus Cadenheid*, in Pitteyot in Fetteresso, recorded his own Will. He died on 12th June, 1613, and the Inventory of his estate, amounting to £2105 13s. 4d. Scots, was recorded in the Register of the Commissariot of St. Andrews, Testaments, Vol. 5.

He had sixteen work oxen, "ten ky newkit and furroch with thair followaris—four quoyis, thrie steirs —tua auld hors, seuenty one wedderis—sixty youis" and other sheep. He had a considerable sum of money lent to various persons, amongst others four hundred

merks to "Alexander Bannerman of Elsik." He owed
small sums to Thomas Burnett in Brathinche and
Andro Burnett in "Nuk" and to *Janet Caldenheid* in
Findown. His spouse Catherine Jak and Abraham
Forfar his sisters son were named his executors. A
life-rent of most of his estate was given to his wife.
John and *Andro Caldenheid* are mentioned as his
brothers, and to them and his sisters the fee of his
estate was left. Amongst the legacies there is "to
tua sisters barnes ane lad and ane las callit craigis ilk
ane of them ten merkis."

This is evidently the Will of a childless and probably
elderly man, who may have been contemporary with
or one generation later than Mrs. Gilbert Rait.

In this year an Obligation is recorded in the Sheriff
Court Books of Aberdeenshire on 20th May, 1616, by
James Curour in Kinmunite as principal, and Alex-
ander Robertson, Minister at Aboyne, Alexander
Curour in Kinmunite, and George Gordon in Wood-
end of Birse, Cautioners for 200 merks. The witnesses
are George Seton of Schethin ; William Dunn, Muir-
town of Bourtie ; *Magnus Cadonheid*, son to *Andrew
Cadonheid* in Cortanes of Drum ; Andrew Murray, son
to Thomas Murray, Burgess, Aberdeen ; and Andrew
Clark, Procurator. The deed was written by *Magnus
Cadonheid.* This seems to make *Andrew* in Cortanes

of Drum contemporary with Magnus in Pitteyot, and it is not improbable that he was the brother Andrew mentioned in his Will.

1633   In the Spalding Club Miscellany, Vol. III., p. 116, the Laird of Drum is noted as debtor, in 1633, to *Magnus Caddenheid* in Cortanes, in the sum of one thousand merks.

1634   The oldest gravestone in Drumoak Churchyard, a large slab of pink Hill-of-Fare granite, with the lettering and carving in relief, records that—"Here lyes *Androw Cadenheid* in Drummoake who depairted 27 Decer. 1634; and Isobel Gray his Spovs, who depairted the [illegible]. In all things remember the end."

It will now be more convenient to give the names according to the localities where they appear :—

FETTERESSO.

1620   Robert Caddenheid was married to Marion Corlens in Dunnoter.

John Caddenheid had "barne" baptized.

Catharin Caddenheid and R. Veitche were married.

1623   John Caddenheid had a child baptized.

1626   John Caddenheid in Muchels ane barne baptized called Magnus; witness Magnus Caddenheid in Dilmoak; and other children.

1628 John Caddenheid, witness to baptism of child of Magnus Tailzeour.

1630 Magnus Mylne in Fetteresso, and Barbara Caddenhcid in Dilmayock, married.

1633 John Caddenheid, Skipper in Muchels, witness to a baptism.

1637 James Caddenheid and Christian Clark married.

John Caddenheid and Isa. Broune married.

1638 Thomas Mitchell and Janet Caddenheid married.

Robert Caddenheid in Muchels, witness to a baptism.

1641 Robert Caddenheid and John Caddenheid, witnesses to a baptism.

Patrik Gray in Peterculter, and Margaret Caddenheid in Fetteresso, married.

John Caddenheid, younger, in Muchels, had a child baptized.

1657 Robert Cadinhed and Kathren Souter married.

1675 The Will of Margaret Cadonheid, at the Mill of Monqueich, in Fetteresso—recorded by George Mowat at the said Mill, Magnus Millne and John Millne her sons, and Wm. Schipherd in Auquhortes her nearest of kin. Reg. of Commissariot of St. Andrews, Vol. 13. 3. July.

ARBUTHNOTT.

1634   Allexr. Cadinheid presented ane child to be baptized Androwe.

1635   Alexr. Cadinheid and Agnes Eltine married.

1637   Alexr. Cadinheid had a child baptized Christane—witnesses, John Young and Alexr. Cadinheid in Boghall.

Andrew Wise and Kristan Kaddinheid in Mongoudrum were married.

1638   Alexr. Kaddinheid had a child baptized Kirstan—witnesses, Robert Arbuthnot in Lonheid, and Robert Arbuthnot in Kirktown.

1639   Alexr. Cadonheid had a child baptized George.

Dec. 24, 1640   Alexr. Cadinheid had a child baptized Alexander.

Jan. 19, 1642   Alexr. Kaddinheid in Allardes had a child baptized Kirstan.

1660   Robert Welsh in Kineff, and Barbara Cadinheid, married.

1662   George Cadinhead in Old Caike, and Margaret Hill, married.

1665   George Cadinhead in Kair had ane soune baptized George.

1669   Alexr. Cran and Katheren Cadinhead, both in East Bamfe, married.

1677   Francis Hill and Margt. Cadinhead married.

1702   David Cadenhead had a son baptized John.

1708   David Cadenhead and Mary Hill married.

1714   Alexr. Birss, servant to the Earll of Hyndfoord, and Elspet Cadenhead, servitrix to the Viscount Arbuthnott, married.

1717   John Caldenhead, servant to Pitcarles, and Helen Coutts, married. Cautioners for the man, Thomas Allardes in Pitcarles ; and, for the woman, Alexr. Robertson in Dunream.

1725   John Cadenhead in Auchindreach had a son baptized William; and in 1727 and 1728 sons, James and Alexander.

1727   David Cadenhead in Pitcarles buried.

1736   David Cadenhead and Anne Birss married.

1737   David Cadenhead in Deep had a child baptized Katherine.

1743   Alexr. Cadenhed in Old Cake buried.

1744   Alexr. Cadenhead and Elspet Stuart married.

1750   Anne Cadenhead, infant daughter of Alexr. Cadenhead in Pitcarles, buried.

1756   Margaret Allardice in Pitcarles, Relict of Alexr. Cadenhead, buried.

1757   Elspet Stewart, spouse to Alexr. Cadenhead in Pitcarles, buried.

Alexander Cadenhead and Isabel Torn married.

1758   David, a child of Alexander Cadenhead in Pitcarles, buried.

1766   Alexander Cadenhead in Elpity buried.

Margaret Cadenhead in Bamfhill buried.

1773   David Cadenhead in Redheugh in ffordon buried.

1775   James Cadenhead in Kinkell of Fordon, a young man, buried.

KINNEFF.

1619   Archibald Cadenheid haid a dochter baptis'd Barbara.

1644   James Fiddas and Barbra Cadenheid married.

1646   They had a child baptized John.

1657   Robert Cadinhead of Fetteresso Parish, and Kathren Souter, married.

1667   John Moncur and Catharin Cadinhead to receive testimoniells.

1668   Alexander Cathenhead to receive a testimoniall.

1672   Androw Catinhead in Fetteresso Parish, and Margt. Watt, married.

1678   Alexr. Cadenhead in the Parish of Caterline, and Barbara Usher, married.

BANCHORY DEVENICK.

1624   William Moscrope and Janet Cadinheid married.

1695   ALEXANDER CADDENHEID in Wastertoune of Pitfoddels paid the poll tax for himself and his wife,

Margaret Knolls; also for servant Elspet Knolls. At same time Magnus Knolls was tenant in Mains of Cults and paid poll tax. See Peterculter, 1738.

1695 George Cadenheid, servant to Robert Irvine of Coultes, paid poll tax.

1731 William Cadenhead in Peter-Culter, and Margaret Harrow, married.

1744 William Cadenhead in Kemhill had a daughter Isobel baptized.

DRUMOAK.

1649 & 1653 John Caddenheid in Lochsyde is a party to two actions in the Sheriff Court of Aberdeen.

1655 Janet Cadonheid, now spous to Robert Burnet in Drummock, takes a Bond from Alexander Gordon, weaver, burges of Aberdeen, that he has received the yairne of twa pairs of fingering plaids, which he bound himself his heirs and executors to restore and deliver in sufficient woivine wark to the said Janet betwixt that date and Pasche next, failing which, twentie merks Scots money for each plaid— and he also granted him to be due the said Janet and her spouse the sum of twenty-four merks.

1656 Jannet Caddenhead, relict of the deceased Robert Bannerman, sometyme in Drummoak, and Robert Burnet, now her spouse, for his interest, along with William Davidson of Carnie, and Jean

Abercromby his spouse, are summoned by Sir Alexander Irving of Drum to remove from the lands of Drummoak and Pitbranzean.

1668 Janet Cadenhed, still in Drummoak, grants an obligation to Robert Patrie of Portlethen, Provost of Aberdeen, for threescoir and four marks Scots. The document in the Sheriff Clerk's archives shows that Janet's signature was that of an educated lady ; and Robert Bannerman, presumably her son, who witnessed the deed, writes like a scribe.

ST. NICHOLAS PARISH.

1563 William Cadenheid, Fisherman in Futtie, was infeft in three "domunculas contigue coadjacentes" in Futtie—and these properties descended to his son David, his grandsons Archibald and Robert, his great-grandson Richard, his great-great-grandson John, his great-great-great-grandsons Robert and John ; and, in 1734, to his great-great-great-great-grand-daughters Margaret, Marjorie and Isobel, all married women.

1641
1646 Alexander Caddinghead and Janet Cruickshank had children Christian and Alexander baptized—the former by Mr. Andrew Cant.

1654 John Caddenhead and Marjorie Wanhaggan had a child Richard baptized, and five others—Peter, Christian, John, Sybbell and Alexander—down to 1663.

1664　John Caddenhead and Helen Brown were married, and thereafter had children William and Isobell baptized.

1672　John Cadenhead and Elspet Lessell had, between that and 1679, six children—Robert, Andrew, Jean, James and Elspet—baptized.

1683　John Cadenheid, horsehirer, and Janet Henderson, had a child John baptized, and five others—Elspet, Christian, Margaret, Janet and Isabel—down to 1692.

1695　Alexander Cadenhead, servant to William Shipperd, roapmaker, poll taxed on £10 wages.

John Cadenhead, with Patrick Gellie, late bailie, poll taxed on £20 wages.

John Cadenhead, horsehirer, poll taxed for himself, wife, and child, Christian.

1754　Moses Cadinghead, sailor, had a son Alexander baptized.

1758　James Cadinghead, warkman, and Isabel Guild, had a son John baptized, and six others—James, William, Isabel, James, Helen and Margaret—down to 1773.

1762　Moses Cadenhead, designed as midshipman on board His Majesty's Navy, purchased a large ancient house in Shiprow for himself and Margaret Calder his spouse, in conjunct fee and liferent, and in 1771 he gave a Power of Attorney to William Burnett, Advocate in Aberdeen, on the narrative that by his way of life and frequent residence in foreign parts he cannot personally attend to the management of his affairs—under which power Mr. Burnett sold the property in 1782.

1765   Alexander Cadenhead, gardener, and Margaret Martin at Windmillbrae, married.

1766   They had a son William baptized, and five thereafter—James, Agnes, James, William and Robert—down to 1784.

1789   "Mr. George Cadenhead and Mrs. Margaret Mountford," his wife, had a son Smith baptized by the Rev. John Skinner, Bishop.

TORRIE.

1623   Andrew Caddonheid is witness to a sasine of Alexander Gairdyne of Banchorie Devenick of the sunny half of the lands of the Barony of Torrie.

1624   Adam Caddonheid, Miller at the Mill of Kincorthe, is witness to a Sasine of Gilbert Menzies of Pitfoddels of the half Barony of Torrie.

1625 & 1628   The said Andrew is a witness to other two Sasines.

1636   Margaret, Janet and Jean Caddonheids, lawful sisters and co-heirs of the late David Caddonheid, son of the late Andrew Caddonheid, indweller in Torrie, and Bessie Craighead his wife, are infeft in a property in Torrie.

MARYCULTER.

1699　John Cadonhead in Blairs and in Auchlunies, and Agnes Galloway, had a son William baptized, and three others—Jean, Margaret and Isobel—in 1701, 1703, and 1706.

1709　Alexander Shepherd in Wester Tilbouries and in Bennagubs, and Rebekkah Cadonhead, had a daughter Jean baptized, and five others—Rebekkah, Isobel, Alexander, Margaret and Agnes—in 1714, 1716, 1719, 1720, and 1725.

1717　Robert Duthie in Tilbouries, and Christian Caddenhead, had a son Robert baptized.

SKENE.

1726　Alexander Cadonhead in Easter Kinmundy had two children baptized Margaret and Elizabeth.

1748　George Grig in Easter Kinmundy, and Margaret Cadonhead, had a daughter Margaret baptized.

1750　The said George and his wife had twins, Alexander and John, baptized.

DUNNOTTAR.

1706　John Caddonhead in Stonehaven had a son Alexander baptized.

1708　The said John had a daughter Margaret baptized.

C

PETERCULTER.

1719   ALEXANDER CADENHEAD in Stengavel, son of Alex-
       ander in Westertown of Pitfoddels (see Banchory-
       Devenick, 1695), had a son baptized ALEXANDER.

1720   He had a son baptized John.

1722   He had a daughter baptized Jean.

172–   He had a son baptized William.

1723   George Cadenhead in Binghill had a son baptized
       Alexander.

1724   He had a son baptized Robert.

1731   George Cadenhead in Peterculter, and Katherine Lay
       in Banchory Ternan, were married.

       William Cadenhead in Peterculter, and Margaret
       Harrow in Banchory Devenick, were married.

1732   William Cadenhead in Windyhills had a son baptized
       James.

1735   Same man, then in Mains of Culter, had a son baptized
       William.

1739   He had a son baptized John.

1732   Elspet Donald, aged 51, spouse of John Caddonhead,
       buried in Peterculter Churchyard (grave-stone).

1736   Robert Cadenhead in Glasterberry had a daughter Ann
       baptized.

1738   Margaret Knolls, aged 72, spouse of ALEXANDER
       CADDANHEAD, buried in Peterculter Churchyard.

1740 John Cadenhead in Nether Cantley had a son baptized
John.

1741 Robert Cadenhead in Robertstown had a son
baptized Alexander ;
in 1744 a son   „   John ;
in 1746 a son   „   Robert.

1742 John Cadenhead in Lochtown, thereafter in East
Eddiestown, had a son baptized John ;
in 1749 a daughter   „   Dorothea ;
in 1756 a daughter   „   Mary.

1750 ALEXANDER CADENHEAD in Westfield and ――――
Aitken had a son baptized (1) JOHN ;
in 1754 a son   „   (2) William ;
in 1756 a son   „   (3) Alexander ;
in 1759 a daughter   „   (4) Helen.
(1) married Anna Bonner, and had issue. (2)
William, m. Margaret Duncan, and had issue.
(3) studied medicine—went to West Indies—died
unmarried at New Providence, 1801. (4) died in
old age unmarried.

1760 William Cadenhead in Blackton, and afterwards Mains
of Countesswells, a son of Alexander in Stengavel, had (1) in 1760 a daughter Helen ; (2) in
1761 a daughter Margaret; (3) in 1763 a daughter
Isobel ; (4) in 1765 a son John ; and (5) in 1767
a daughter Janet.

These four daughters all died unmarried. John
(4) held a commission as Lieutenant in the Corps
of Gilcomston Pikemen of the Volunteers of the

North in 1803; being an elder of Gilcomston Chapel of Ease, and having on one occasion sent a gift of potatoes to the minister, that gentleman, the Rev. Dr. Kidd, acknowledged the gift in his next Sunday's sermon by telling his people that they were all black at the heart like his friend John Cadenhead's potatoes. He married in 1809 Isobel Sim, daughter of James Sim, brewer in Aberdeen, sister of Duncan Sim, afterwards Lieutenant-General in the Royal Engineers, and had issue (1) in 1809 a son Duncan; (2) in 1811 a son John; (3) in 1814 a son James; and (4) in 1816 a daughter Helen.

Duncan (1) died in Calcutta unmarried. John (2) was an M.D., held a medical appointment in the East India Company's service in the Madras Presidency, was also Deputy Commissioner at Orissa Goomsoor, and founded schools there; married Charlotte Helen Davidson, and had issue, four daughters—Louisa, Florence, Edith & Jessie. James (3) married Anne, daughter of Alexander Cadenhead, Advocate in Aberdeen, and had issue (See Appendix). Helen (4) died young, unmarried.

1762　Robert Cadenhead in Robertstown, probably son of Robert in Robertstown in 1746, probably son of George in Binghill in 1723, twice married. Had issue by first marriage—(1) Robert in 1762; (2) George in 1764; (3) William in 1767. By second marriage—(4) Alexander in 1773; and (5) James in 1775.

George (2) was an excise officer, had a son Robert, sometime merchant in Glasgow, now in America, whose son Thomas was killed by the natives while acting as a leader of a Royal Belgian exploring expedition in Western Africa in 1880.

James (5) died in Aberdeen, aged 93, and had issue—Peter, shipmaster, William, wine merchant, and others.

Tradition indicates this family to have been related to the family in Stengavel, probably one degree more remotely than the family in Cantley.

1773   John Cadenhead in Upper Cantley married Agnes Smith ; died 16 June, 1806, aged 63. Had issue in 1773 a daughter Agnes ; in 1775 a daughter Dorothy ; and in 1777 a son William.

The said son William married Agnes Pirie, and died in Upper Cantley 16 Dec., 1841, aged 63, leaving issue—William, Margaret, John, Nancy, George and Dorothea. The family is still in Cantley.

Mrs. Benjamin Reid's tradition, above-quoted, goes on to say that her great-grandfather, Alexander Cadenhead in Stengavel, and John in Upper Cantley in 1773, were first-cousins. The tombstone of the Cantley family in Peterculter lies next to that bearing the name of Margaret Knolls, the wife of Alexander in Westerton of Cults (Banchory Devenick) in 1695. Elspet Donald and John Caddonhead on the same stone may be the ancestors of the Cantley family.

OLD MACHAR.

1781   William Cadenhead in Windmillbrae, and Margaret
       Duncan, were married, and had issue :—
       in 1782 a daughter baptized Elizabeth ;
       in 1785 a son   „   Alexander ;
       in 1787 a daughter   „   Mary ;
       in 1789 a daughter   „   Margaret ;
       in 1792 a son   „   William ;
       in 1793 a son   „   John ;
       in 1794 a son   „   William.

   Note.—John, physician in Aberdeen, married
   Jessie Duguid—left no issue. Margaret married
   Benjamin Reid—left no issue. The others died
   unmarried.

William Cadenhead in Scotstown, and Jean Smith,
   had a daughter baptized Helen ;
   in 1783 a son   „   Thomas ;
   in 1785 a son   „   William.

1784   JOHN CADENHEAD in Old Machar, and Anna Bonner in
       Nigg, were married, thereafter had issue baptized
       in 1786 a son   (1) ALEXANDER, married JANE
       in 1787 a daughter (2) Anne ;   [SHIRREFS ;
       in 1789 a daughter (3) Barbara ;
       in 1792 a son   (4) John ;
       in 1795 a daughter (5) Anne.

LONDON.

1804   Moses Cadenhead. — Probate of his will issued, designed "late of the City of London, now of the Parish of St. Anns, in the County of Middlesex mariner." His executors were his wife, Frances Ann Cadenhead, David Troup and Jessy Russell, both of the City of London, and Robert Cadenhead, of the Parish of Trelawney, and Thomas Winder, of the Parish of St. Ann, in the island of Jamaica. He had a brother James, a sister Jane, and his sons, minors, were Jessy, David and Alexander. The witnesses were James Newby, Alexander Cadenhead and John Christie.

MISCELLANEOUS CADENHEADS.

1558   A gift under the privy seal was made in favour of Issobell Caddounheid hir airis assignais ane ar ma of the moveable gudis quhilkis pertenit to umquhill Gilbert Young. The domiciles of the deceased and the grantee are not mentioned.

1561   William Cadenheid convicted (in the High Court of Justiciary) for art and part the theftuous steling of ane black cut tailit horse fra the Erll Marshell and ane gray horse fra James Andersoun ; quhairwith he was tane reid-hand. Hanged on ye gallowse of the Burrow Mure. The *locus delicti* and domicile of the accused are not mentioned.

1577   In the ecclesiastical records of Aberdeen it appears
that James Cadenheid and Jonet Ailhous were (for
their sins) ordained to sitt with paper crowns at the
Cross and thereafter married.

1613   In the said records it appears that Violett Cadenhead, spouse of William Walker in Futtie, was found
guilty of calling her sister Annabell ane manifest witch.
These were grandchildren of William, who purchased
the three "domunculas" in 1563. The imputation was
a dangerous one, for only sixteen years previously
Thomas Leys, Janet Wischert, Isobel Cocker and
Isobell Monteithe had been tried and convicted of
sorcerie and witchcraft, and of "dansin with the dewill,
at the mercat and fish cross of Aberdene, under the
conduct and gyding of the dewill, playing before them
on his kynd of instruments"; and the three first-named
had been burned at the Cross on 23 February, 1597,
with "twenty loads of peattis, ane boll of coillis and
four tar barrellis"; while the last-named, "quha hangit
herself in prison," had cost the Treasurer of Aberdeen
ten shillings "for trailling her through the streits of
the toun in ane cart and eirding (burying) of her."

ANNA BONNER,

Wife of John Cadenhead.

As far back as the parish records of Nigg in
Kincardineshire reach, there appear several families
of Bonner in the Barony of Torrie, but a blank from

1693 to 1718 prevents this genealogy from being articulately traced beyond—

Andrew Bonner, who was session clerk and schoolmaster in 1726. He married (1st), in 1728, Jean Marnoch, daughter of Alexander Marnoch, farmer in Kirkhill, and had by her six sons and two daughters. He married (2nd), on 14th July, 1752, Katherine Low, daughter of the deceased Alexander Low, portioner in Inverurie, and had issue in 1753 (1) Katherine; on 14th June, 1755 (2), ANNA; in 1758 (3) Barbara; and in 1760 (4) Sophia. He died on 9th April, 1787, aged 85.

Katherine (1) married George Smith, whence families of Duncan, Allan, Linklater and others. Barbara (3) married James Donald, excise officer, whose daughter Katherine married —— Bremner, Wick, and had issue.

JANE SHIRREFS,

Wife of Alexander Cadenhead.

I. William Shirrefs, in Balfour of Putachie, anno 16—, had one son.

II. James Shirrefs, in Little Miln of Forbes, married Christian Blair, and had one son.

III. Alexander Shirrefs, in Drumnagour of Kildrummy (fought at Sheriff-muir on the Stuart side, was captured and kept prisoner four months at

Carlisle), had issue by first marriage (1) John ;
(2) James ; (3) William ; (4) Alexander ; (5)
Duncan ; (6) Alexander ; (7) David ; and a
daughter.

IV. David Shirrefs, builder in Aberdeen, married,
21 December, 1748, Jane Lunan, and had issue
(1) John, died in infancy; (2) James; (3) David,
planter in Jamaica, left no issue ; (4) Mary,
died unmarried ; (5) Barnet, died unmarried ;
(6) Anne, died unmarried ; (7) Alexander,
advocate in Aberdeen, married Anne Gordon,
through whom his grandson succeeded to the
lands of Craig; (8) Andrew, bookseller and
poet, died unmarried; (9) Thomas; (10) Robert;
(11) Jane, married John Smith, advocate in
Aberdeen, left no issue.

V. James Shirrefs, D.D., one of the ministers of the
West Church, Aberdeen, married, 28 Sept., 1790,
Amelia, tenth daughter of James Morison, of
Disblair and Elsick, Esquire, and Provost of
Aberdeen, and had issue (1) David in 1791,
died unmarried ; (2) James in 1793, died un-
married; (3) Alexander in 1794, died unmarried;
(4) Amelia in 1796, married Robert Burnett,
W.S., and had a large family ; (5) JANE on 17
Dec., 1797, married ALEXANDER CADENHEAD.

AMELIA MORISON,

Wife of James Shirrefs, D.D.

I. James Morison, merchant and Provost of Aberdeen,
1731-2; born 1665; died Feb., 1748; married,
29 March, 1692, Anna Low in Old Aberdeen, had
issue five sons and three daughters.

II. James Morison (fifth son of the above J. M.), of
Elsick, Provost of Aberdeen, 1745-6 and 1752-3;
baptized 25 Aug., 1708; died 5 Jan., 1786; married
Isobel Dyce, eldest daughter of James Dyce of
Disblair, merchant in Aberdeen, and had five sons:

(1) James M., baptized 20 April, 1741.

(2) Wm. Augustus M., baptized 8 August, 1746.

(3) Thomas M., of Elsick and Disblair, M.D.,
baptized 15 August, 1749; died unmarried.

(4) Alexander M., baptized 14 Nov., 1753.

(5) George M., D.D., of Elsick and Disblair;
and eleven daughters—

(1) Agnes M., baptized 16 June, 1734; married,
17 June, 1754, Robert Farquhar of New-
hall, Kincardineshire, merchant stationer in
Aberdeen, had a large family, *inter alios*
the late Major-Gen. William F., Admiral
Sir Arthur F., &c.

(2) Anne M., baptized 1 Feb., 1738; married 1st Rev. John Farquhar, minister of Nigg, brother of Sir Walter Farquhar, *s.p.*; and 2nd, 24 Dec., 1777, Rev. Alexander Mearns, minister of Towie, thereafter of Cluny, and had issue—the late Rev. Duncan Mearns, D.D.

(3) Isobell M., baptized 24 July, 1739; married, 9 Dec., 1787, James Abercrombie of Bellfield, Kincardineshire, *s.p.*

(4) Mary M., baptized 22 Dec., 1742; married Rev. John Hutcheon, minister of Fetteresso; died Aug., 1775, leaving issue—the late David H., Advocate in Aberdeen, and Mrs. Professor Paul.

(5) Jean M., baptized 26 May, 1744; married Robert Hamilton, LL.D., Marischal Coll., Aberdeen; died *s.p.*

(6) Janet M., baptized 23 Nov., 1747; married, 14 June, 1770, Arthur Dingwall Fordyce of Culsh, LL.D., Commissary of Aberdeen— had a large family; died 15 July, 1831.

(7) Katharine M., bapt. 11 Aug., 1750; married Rev. D. Forbes, minister of Laurencekirk, and had issue; died, his widow, 22 October, 1820.

(8) Rachel M., baptized 12 Aug., 1752; died unmarried.

(9) Helen M., baptized 16 Dec., 1754; died unmarried.

(10) AMELIA M., baptized 21 Jan., 1756; married, 28 Oct., 1790, Rev. JAMES SHIRREFS, D.D.

(11) Sophia M., baptized 19 August, 1760; died unmarried.

MARY BURNETT,

Wife of John Lunan.

Sir Thomas Burnett of Leys, 1st Baronet, married (1st) Margaret, daughter of Sir Robert Douglas of Glenbervie, and had issue (1) Alexander, whence the line of Leys; (2) Robert, born 1610, Advocate 1642, married Cath. Pearson, daughter of Lord Southhall; (3) Jean, married, 1632, Sir William Forbes, 2nd Bart. of Monymusk; (4) Katherine, married, 1638, Robert Gordon of Pitlurg.

He married (2nd), in 1621, Jane, daughter of Sir Thomas Moncrieff of Moncrieff, and widow of Sir Simon Fraser of Inverallochy, and had issue (1) Thomas; (2) William; (3) James, in Russia, 1659-67; (4) Elizabeth, married (1st) Sir Robert Douglas of Tilquhilly, (2nd) Fullerton of Kinaldie; and five other daughters.

Thomas Burnett, eldest son of said second marriage, acquired Sauchen by marriage with Bessie, elder

daughter and co-heiress of William Burnett, parson
of Kinnerny, and had issue (1) Robert; (2) William; (3) Alexander.

Robert Burnett (1) of Sauchen, *vita patris* parson,
first of Banchory, afterwards of Fintray, married,
in or before 1681, Jane Reid, and had issue (1)
Robert; (2) John; (3) ? Janet, mar. Thomas Reid.

Robert Burnett (1) of Sauchen had issue (1)
Robert of Sauchen, who married Jane Barclay,
and had issue; (2) Andrew, surgeon in Old Aberdeen, who married Anna Burnett; (3) Catharine,
married Robert Calder; (4) MARY, married JOHN
LUNAN.

JANE LUNAN,

Wife of David Shirrefs.

Note.—The history of the family of Montealto,
and the change of the name through the Norman-French Mont-haut into Mowat is well known. In
1242 Richard Montealt was a Justiciary of Scotland, and had a son who was Abbot of Arbroath.
In 1262 to 1266 William and Robert Montalt
were Sheriffs of Forfar, and Lawrence Montealt
was Rector of Kinnettles. In 1289 to 1320
William de Montealto was a leading man in
Scotland.

In 1382 Ricardus de Lownane et Pitfour was
well known to the citizens of Aberdeen. He

owned a mansion in the Gallowgate, and on the occasion of some civil dispute he was chosen as arbiter between the parties. In the Aberdeen records he is sometimes referred to simply as Richard Lownan. A court which had communicated, past his house, between the Gallowgate and the Loch was known till nearly the middle of the 19th century as Lunan's Court. In 1383 Ricardus de Lownan sold his lands of Lownan and Pitfour to Alexander Stewart—a natural son of King Robert II.—and in Stewart's charter of confirmation the name of the seller is found to be Ricardus Mouet. He was successively chaplain, canon and chancellor of Brechin cathedral.

In 1435 Dominus Laurencius Lownane had built a new school in Dundee, without leave from the Bishop, and was rebuked.

In 1436 a Notary Public, a Canon of Dunkeld, subscribes himself Walterus de Lownane.

In 1450 a John Lownane, a proprietor in the Apilgate of Arbroath, is a chaplain of Brechin.

In 1480 a Thomas Lunane is proprietor of Mongallie, and 163 years later there is a William Lunan in the same place.

In 1544 Agnes Lownan is the wife of Thomas Strathauchin, *civis civitatis Abredonensis.*

In 1544 Frater Duncanus Lownan is one of the Conventus of Deir, and subscribes a feu-charter in favour of William, Lord Forbes, and his spouse.

In 1588 Richard Lunan was laureated in Edinburgh University ; and, in 1593, was appointed minister of Marykirk.

Alexander Lunan was, in 1611, entered a student at King's College, Aberdeen; in 1615 he is capped with honours; in 1618 he is Humanist in the University; in 1626 he is Regent, and is also parson of Monymusk. Thereafter he was minister of Kintore; and, in March, 1632, being then parson of Monymusk, he married Jean, eldest daughter of Sir William Forbes of Monymusk, and had issue one son, viz.:—

William Lunan of Dallob, a notary public, born at Kintore in 1633; died at Abersinthick in April, 1681; married, on 24th Dec., 1663, Barbara daughter of Alexander Gordon of Merdrom, and had issue a son and a daughter—William and Anna.

Anna, born 2nd May, 1669; married, on 8th October, 1685, John Forbes, son of William Forbes of Tombeg, Monymusk; died between Whitsunday, 1741, and Whitsunday, 1742. Her descendants were Forbeses of Baudiefurrow (now Manar), which family ended with an heiress, who married William Johnston, of the old family of Caskieben. The last of whose descendants, a female, died at Calsayseat, near Aberdeen, in 1855, and from whose kinsman, Alexander Johnston, Esquire, W.S., the compiler, received a duplicate of Anna Lunan's marriage contract, a copy of the last receipt granted by her for her annuity of 100 merks Scots in 1741, and access to other documents shewing the history of the family.

William Lunan was born at Dallob on 8th Nov., 1664, and died at Kirkton of Monymusk on 8th January, 1735. He married, on 4th October, 1691, Isobel, daughter of William Thain of Blackhall, who died at Blairdaff in 1739. They had ten children—(1) William in 1692, who married Elspet Thain, sister of Sheriff Thain of Aberdeen ; (2) Jane on 3rd Nov., 1694; (3) Barbara in 1697; (4) John in 1698; (5) Anne 1st in 1699; (6) Margaret in 1701 ; (7) Alexander in 1703, an Episcopal clergyman, died at Inglismaldie ; (8) Mary in 1706 ; (9) James in 1708 ; (10) Anne 2nd in 1710.

John Lunan (4), glazier, burgess of Aberdeen ; married, about 1724, Mary, daughter of Robert Burnett of Sauchen, Esq., and had by her five children—(1) Robert, who died while serving his country in the Royal Navy; (2) JANE on 25 July, 1727, married to DAVID SHIRREFS ; (3) Andrew, who died in Aberdeen ; (4) John, who died in Jamaica ; (5) Anne, who died in Aberdeen, unmarried, in 1802.

BARBARA GORDON,

Wife of William Lunan.

Adam de Gordun, of East and West Gordun, in Berwickshire, killed at the siege of Alnwick on 13 Nov., 1093, was succeeded by

Adam de Gourdon, his son, who was succeeded by

D

Richard de Gordun, who died about 1200, and was
  succeeded by his son,

Thomas de Gordun, who died about 1230, and was
  succeeded by his son,

Thomas De Gordun, who died about 1260, and was
  succeeded by his daughter,

Alicia de Gordun, who married Adam de Gordun,
  her cousin, who accompanied the Earls of Athole
  and Carrick on a crusade, and died at Tunis in
  1269. She was succeeded by her son,

Adam de Gordun, who died about 1295, and was
  succeeded by his son,

Adam de Gordun, who was warden of the marches
  in 1300. He acquired the barony of Strathbolgie,
  and was killed at Hallidon on 19th July, 1333.
  His son William was ancestor of the family of
  Kenmure. His daughter Mary married Sir Walter
  Hambleton of Cadzow, ancestor of the Dukes of
  Hamilton. He was succeeded by his eldest son,

Alexander de Gordun, who was killed at the battle
  of Durham in 1346, and was succeeded by his son,

John de Gordun, who was taken prisoner, along with
  King David I., at the battle of Durham. He
  was succeeded by his son,

John de Gordon, a distinguished soldier, who married
  Elizabeth, daughter of Cruickshanks of Aswanley,
  and was killed at Otterburn on 21st July, 1388.

  He had three sons, viz., (1) Adam de Gordon ;
  (2) John Gordon, known in Scottish tradition as

"Jock Gordon"; (3) Thomas Gordon, known in Scottish tradition as "Tam Gordon." Adam de Gordon (1) married Elizabeth, fourth daughter of Sir William Keith, Great Marischal of Scotland, and had two daughters. His younger daughter having died unmarried, he was succeeded in his great estates of Strathbolgie, and others, by his elder daughter Elizabeth, who married, in 1408, Alexander, son of Sir William Seaton of Seaton, and was ancestress of the Seaton Gordons; whereof the chiefs were Earls and Marquises of Huntly, and Dukes of Gordon.

George, second Earl of Huntly, married the Lady Jean Stewart, daughter of King James I.; and their second son, Sir Adam, having married Lady Elizabeth, heiress of Sutherland, was created Earl of Sutherland.

Thomas Gordon (3) of Davoch, had about eighteen sons, who all, or most of them, founded families of name.

While "Jock and Tam" are by Gordon genealogists represented as the legitimate sons of John de Gordon, they are by others, and at the Lyon office, held to have been his illegitimate sons.

John Gordon (2) (Jock) of Esse and Scurdargue, married Margaret, daughter of Sir P. Maitland of Gight. He died about 1420, and had two sons, viz., John, from whom descends Pitlurg; and

William Gordon of Tillitarmount, who married the daughter of Sir John Rutherford, and had two sons, viz., George, from whom descended the house of Lesmoir; and

Patrick Gordon of Fulziemont (Esslemont), who married Rachel, daughter of Barclay of Towie, and had four sons, viz., William, from whom descended the house of Craig; Patrick, from whom descended the house of Tilliquhoudie, being the second family so designed; Thomas of Corichie; and

George Gordon of Coclarachie, who married a daughter of Oliphant of Berrydales, and had one son,

George Gordon of Coclarachie, who married the daughter and only child of John Gordon of Tilliquhoudie (younger son of Adam Gordon, of Aboyne and Sutherland), heiress; and had one son,

George Gordon of Coclarachie, who married the daughter of James Duncan of Merdrum; and had two sons, viz., George of Coclarachie, and

Alexander Gordon of Merdrum, whose daughter, BARBARA GORDON, married 1st —— Orem; and 2nd WILLIAM LUNAN as aforesaid. He had also a son James, whose three daughters, Margaret, Jeane and Marie, were infeft in New Merdrum in January, 1669.

Note. The Gordon genealogy is historical. The foregoing account, down to, and including John de Gordon and his family, is compiled from "The Gordon Pedigree made out by William Gordon, Esquire, of Harperfield, solicitor-at-law in London, 1781," of which manuscript the compiler has a copy; and from the published "History of the Ancient Noble and Illustrious Family of Gordon, by Mr. William Gordon, of Old Aberdeen, 1726." The descents from John Gordon of Esse and Scurdargue, to Alexander Gordon of Merdrum, are given on the authority of a written statement by the Lyon King-at-Arms, dated 2nd July, 1868, in the compiler's possession.

JEAN FORBES,

Wife of Rev. Alexander Lunan.

James, Second Lord Forbes, by Lady Egidia Keith, his wife, daughter of the first Earl Marischal, had issue three sons.

William (1), from whom the Lords Forbes descend; Duncan (2) of Corsindae; Patrick (3) of Corse.

Duncan Forbes (2) of Corsindae, who married the daughter of Thomas Lumsdaine of Conland, and had two sons—James, his successor in Corsindae, and

Duncan Forbes of Monymusk, who married Agnes, daughter of Baillie William Gray of Aberdeen, had three sons and three daughters. William (1) his heir; John (2); Duncan (3). Isabel (1) married to the Laird of Muchell; Elizabeth (2) married first Barclay of Towie, and second Strachan of Glenkindy; —— (3) married to John Udny of that Ilk.

He died in 1587, succeeded by

William Forbes (1) of Monymusk, who married Lady
Margaret Douglas, daughter of William, ninth
Earl of Angus, by whom he had five sons and
three daughters. William (1) his heir ; John (2),
from whom Forbeses of Leslie; James (3), from
whom Forbeses of Haughton ; Alexander (4) and
Robert (5), who both died without issue. Isabel
(1), married to the Laird of Newton; Elspeth (2);
Margaret (3).

He died before 1618, succeeded by

Sir William Forbes (1) of Monymusk, who married
Elizabeth Wishart, daughter of the Laird of
Pitarrow ; was created a Knight-Baronet of
Nova Scotia, by patent dated 2nd April, 1626,
and had issue three sons and three daughters.
William (1) his heir, from whom descended
the Forbeses of Pitsligo ; Robert (2) of Barnes ;
Alexander (3) of Abersnithack. JEAN (1) mar-
ried to Mr. ALEXANDER . LUNAN, Parson of
Monymusk ; Elizabeth (2) ; and Anne (3).

APPENDIX No. I.

Descents from Issue of Alexander Cadenhead and Jane Shirrefs.

I. Amelia, b. 12 June, 1818 ; d. 10 May, 1852 ; m. 17 June, 1841, Francis Ogston, Professor of Medical Jurisprudence, University of Aberdeen, and had issue (1) Jane ; (2) Alexander ; (3) Francis ; (4) Helen.

(1) Jane, b. 17 July, 1842 ; m. 22 July, 1874, the Rev. Henry Cowan, and had issue— Francis Ogston Cowan, b. 24 Feb., 1877 ; Henry Hargrave Cowan, b. 5 May, 1879 ; Helen Amelia Mary Cowan, b. 31 March, 1881.

(2) Alexander, b. 19 April, 1844 ; m. 1st, 25 Sept., 1867, Mary Jane Hargrave. Issue, Mary Letitia, b. 30 June, 1868 ; Francis Hargrave, b. 18 Aug., 1869 ; Flora Mactavish, b. 1 April, 1872 ; Walter Henry, b. 29 Nov., 1872. 2nd (1 Aug., 1877), Isabella Margaret Matthews. Issue—Alfred James, b. 19 Sept., 1878 ; Helen Charlotte Elizabeth Douglas, b. 10 June, 1883 ; Constance Amelia Irene, b. 25 Oct., 1884; Rosa Fleming, b. 16 June, 1886.

(3) Francis, b. 23 June, 1846 ; m. 30 July, 1879, Charlotte Elizabeth Rhind, who died *s.p.* 12 July, 1883.

(4) Helen Milne, b. 25 April, 1848 ; m. 11 Jan.,
1872, Archibald Edward Malloch, M.D.,
Hamilton, Canada; died *s.p.* 5 Jan., 1873.

IV. Alexander Shirrefs, b. 3 July, 1823 ; died 22 May,
1883 ; m. 31 May, 1850, Mary Arbuthnott
Dingwall Fordyce (grand-daughter of Janet
Morison and Arthur D. F.), and had issue—

(1) Alexander, b. 5 Feb., 1851 ; m. 19 Sept.,
1877, Mary Murray Keefer. Issue—Alexander Dingwall Fordyce, b. Dec., 1878 ;
Mary, b. 23 Jan., 1880; Nelson Keefer,
b. 8 June, 1882 ; Edith, b. 3 Jan., 1884 ;
John Arbuthnott, b. 25 March, 1886.

(2) Arthur, b. 8 Feb., 1853 ; m. 22 Sept., 1883,
Emma Josephine Clark. Issue—Arthur
Fordyce Grant, b. 6 Sept., 1885.

(3) James Shirrefs, b. 16 Feb., 1855; d. 11 Aug.
of same year.

(4) John Arbuthnott, b. 13 Oct., 1857.

(5) Elizabeth, b. 22 January, 1860.

(6) James Brebner, b. 21 Feb., 1862 ; d. 12
Feb., 1864.

(7) George Morison, b. 8 Nov., 1863.

(8) Magdalene Dingwall, b. 27 June, 1866 ; d.
20 August, 1867.

V. Brebner, b. 26 Dec., 1824 ; d. 7 Sept., 1877 ; m. 8
May, 1851, Jane Muir, and had issue—

(1) Alexander George McGillivray (commonly
called George), b. 15 March, 1852.

(2) John, b. 21 Oct., 1853 ; d. 1 March, 1866.

(3) Brebner, b. 4 Aug., 1856.

(4) Jane, b. 17 May, 1860.

(5) James, b. 1 July, 1864.

(6) Thomas Reginald, b. 11 Jan., 1867.

(7) David, b. 3 October, 1869.

VI. George, b. 3 March, 1827 ; m. 10 July, 1855, Katharine Seton Forman Leonard, daughter of James Leonard, Surgeon, London, and had issue,

(1) Alice Jane, b. 7 June, 1856.

(2) James, b. 12 January, 1858.

Alice Jane (1) m. 10 Aug., 1876, William Henry Carter, Merchant, London, and had issue (1) William Leonard, b. 20 May, 1877; (2) George Christopher, b. 29 Dec., 1878 ; (3) Alice Gray, b. 4 Feb., 1880; (4) Stanley Bronislas, b. 19 July, 1882 ; (5) Josephine Elizabeth, b. 25 May, 1886.

VII. Anne, b. 14 Dec., 1829 ; m. 5 Oct., 1854, James Cadenhead, Captain, afterwards Colonel, in the Madras Army, youngest son of John Cadenhead and Isobel Sim, and had issue—

(1) Anne, b. 14 Sept., 1855 ; d. 18 Jan., 1857.

(2) Helen, b. 15 August, 1857.

(3) Emily, b. 27 Sept., 1860 ; d. 30 May, 1876.

(4) James, b. 18 August, 1862.

(5) John, b. 6 August, 1865.

(6) Arthur, b. 16 April, 1870.

APPENDIX No. II.

PRESENTATION TO LEYS BURSARY.

(EXCERPT.)

I Sir Thomas Burnett of Leys Barronett and un-
doubted Patron of the Philosophy and Divinity Burses
aftermentioned To the Principal Masters and Regents
of the Marischall Colledge of Aberdeen Greeting
Forasmuchas The Place of a Philosophy and Divinity
Burse within the said Colledge and the Stipend or
Pension belonging thereto respectively, founded by
Gilbert Lord Bishop of Sarum, Is at present Vacant
and at my Gift and Presentation, And I being most
willing that a Burser and Student of Philosophy and
Divinity be Placed therein And having Information
and Knowledge of the Docility Hope and Good
Expectation of James Shirrefs Lawfull Son to David
Sherriffs Wright in Aberdeen a distant Relation of the
said Lord Bishop of Sarum and of his proficiency in
the Latine Tongue and other Literature Therefore
wit ye me To have nominated and presented Likeas
I by these Presents Nominate and Present The said
James Sheriffs To be Bursar and Student of Philosophy
in the said Colledge &c.

THO. BURNETT.

13 May 1766.

APPENDIX No. III.

THE TRADE OF GLAZIER.

(EXCERPT.)

LYON OFFICE,
EDINBURGH, 25 May, 1868.

The Trade of a "Glazier" "vitrarius" seems to have been formerly in more honour than in later times. About the time of the Reformation I find not merely sons of the principal burgesses, but sometimes of our smaller county families, so designed.

GEORGE BURNETT,
Lyon.

GEORGE CADENHEAD, Esq.

APPENDIX No. IV.

THE BURNETTS OF SAUCHEN.

(EXCERPT.)

LYON OFFICE,
EDINBURGH, 25 May, 1868.

DEAR SIR,

The Burnetts of Sauchen sprang from a younger son of the 1st Baronet of Leys. I have no reason to think any male descendant of this branch exists. The great grand-daughter of the last laird of Sauchen, heir female of the family, is now wife of the Rev. William Polson of Weems (son of the late John Polson, Innkeeper and Stabler, Old Aberdeen). The subjoined sketch, if not very complete, rests on authentic evidence.

Yours faithfully,

GEORGE BURNETT,
Lyon.

1st Wife.
2nd Wife.

Margaret, daughter of Sir Robert Douglas = Sir Thomas Burnett of Leys, = Jane, daughter of Sir Thomas Moncrieff of of Glenbervie.
1st Bart.
Moncrieff, and widow of Sir Simon Fraser of Inverallochy.

- **Alexander,** continued the Line of Leys.
- **Robert,** b. 1610; Advocate, 1642; m. Catherine Pearson, daughter of Lord South-hall.
- **Jean,** married 1642, Sir William Forbes of Monymusk.
- **Katherine,** married 1638, Robert Gordon of Pitlurg.
- **William.**
- *Thomas of Sauchen,* which he acquired by marriage with Bessie, elder daughter and co-heir of William Burnett, parson of Kinnerny.
- **James,** in Russia, 1659-67 (Gen. Gordon's Diary).
- **Elizabeth,** mar. 1st Sir Robert Douglas of Tilquhilly; 2nd Fullerton of Kinaldie.
- Other married daughters.

From Thomas of Sauchen:

- **William.**
- *Robert of Sauchen,* vita patris parson 1st of Banchory, afterwards Fintray, m. in or before 1681, Jane Reid. 1699, served to his father.
- **Alexander.**

From Robert of Sauchen:

- **John.**
- *Robert of Sauchen,* 1713, Sas. on Pr. Cl. C. to his father.
- (?) **Janet,** mar. Thomas Reid.

From Robert of Sauchen:

- **Andrew,** Surgeon, Old Aberdeen, mar. Anna Burnett.
- **Catherine,** mar. Robert Calder.
- **Mary,** mar. John Lunan.
- *Robert of Sauchen,* mar., 1736, Jane, daughter of George Barclay in Esslie.
- **Janet.**

Next generation:

- **Jane.**
- **Margaret,** mar. Jas. Martin, Merchant, Rotterdam.
- **Mary.**
- **Catherine,** mar. David Scott, factor, Craigievar.

APPENDIX No. V.

THE GORDONS OF MERDRUM.

(EXCERPT.)

LYON OFFICE,
EDINBURGH, 2 July, 1868.

DEAR SIR,

I am now able to give you information that can be depended on about Alexander Gordon of Merdrum. The daughter and heir of James Duncan of Merdrum married George Gordon of Coclarachie, and Merdrum went to their second son, the same who so scandalized the Presbytery of Strathbogie. The subjoined pedigree will explain Coclarachie's descent.

Yours faithfully,

GEORGE BURNETT,
Lyon.

GEO. CADENHEAD, Esq.

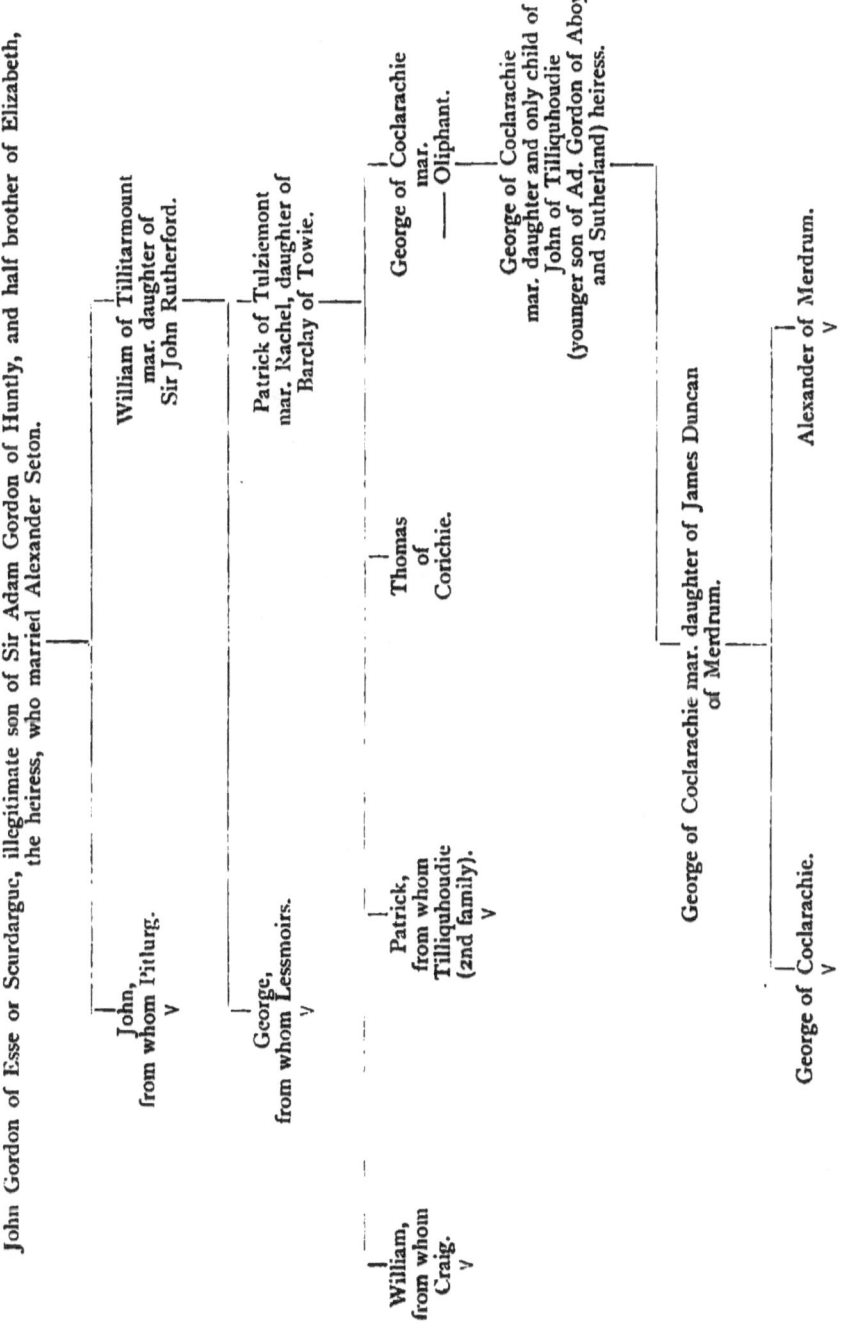

John Gordon of Esse or Scurdarguc, illegitimate son of Sir Adam Gordon of Huntly, and half brother of Elizabeth, the heiress, who married Alexander Seton.

John, from whom Pitlurg. v

William of Tillitarmount mar. daughter of Sir John Rutherford.

George, from whom Lessmoirs. v

Patrick of Tulziemont mar. Rachel, daughter of Barclay of Towie.

Thomas of Corichie.

George of Coclarachie mar. —— Oliphant.

George of Coclarachie mar. daughter and only child of John of Tilliquhoudie (younger son of Ad. Gordon of Aboyne and Sutherland) heiress.

George of Coclarachie mar. daughter of James Duncan of Merdrum.

George of Coclarachie. v

Alexander of Merdrum. v

Patrick, from whom Tilliquhoudie (2nd family). v

William, from whom Craig. v

APPENDIX No. VI.

THE THAINS OF BLACKHALL.

(EXCERPT.)

LYON OFFICE,
EDINBURGH, 25 May, 1868.

Blackhall (parish of Inverury) belonged to the Blackhalls of that Ilk from an early period, with the office of coroner and forester of the Garioch attached to the lands. Early in the 17th century the family seem to have been in difficulties. Alexander Blackhall of that Ilk in 1610, with consent of Leslie of Balquhain, his interdictor, conveyed Blackhall with the coroner and forestership to Alexander Blackhall of Barra, a cadet, whose mother was a Burnett of Leys, reserving the liferent of Janet Strachan, widow of his cousin, to whom he had succeeded. The last Blackhall, I think, who owned the lands, served to his father in 1645 : the lands were alienated (I have not a note of the date) to one —— Thain, whose family held them for some generations. William Thain of Blackhall, afterwards designed " of Melvinside," sold Blackhall to one —— Grant about 1725.

GEORGE BURNETT,
Lyon.

GEORGE CADENHEAD, Esq.

APPENDIX No. VII.

LUNAN GENEALOGIES.

COPY OF A MANUSCRIPT, the first part of which is in the handwriting of John Lunan ; the *italicised* clauses are in that of his son-in-law, Dr. James Shirrefs. The second part of the MS. is wholly in Dr. Shirrefs' handwriting.

Mr. Alex. Lunan, minister of Kintore, was married to Jean Forbes, Lawfull Daughter to Sir Wm. Forbes of Monymusk, in March, 1632.

And had by her one son William, was born in Kintore, 1633.

Said William Lunan was married to Barbara Gordon, daughter of Alexr. Gordon of Merdrum, in Dec. 24th, 1663.

And hade by her, born in Dallob, her first sone William Lunan, 8th Nov., 1664.

And a Daughter Ann, born on 2nd May, 1669.

The said William Lunan died in Abersnithack, Aprile, 1681.

William Lunan, his son, was married to Isobel Thain, Daughter to William Thain of Blackhall, 4th Oct., 1691.

And hade by hir children as followis—

Their first child William was born in the Kirk-town of Monymusk, 1692.

Their 2nd child Jean was born Nov. 3rd, 1694.

Their 3rd Barbra, 1697.

Their 4th John—*Grandfather of the Shirrefs',* 1698.

Their 5th a first Ann, 1699.

Their 6th Margrat, 1701.

Their 7th Alexr., 1703.
An Episcopal Clergyman, died at Inglismaldie.

Their 8th Mary, 1706.

Their 9th James, 1708.

Their 10th Ann, 1710.
Married to N. Cruickshank, died in Aberdeen.

The said William Lunan died in Kirk Town, Monymusk, Jany. 8th, 1735.

And his wife, Isobel Thain in Blairdaff, in 1739.

William, his son, was married to Elspet Thain, sister to Shirref Thain.

[What follows is all in the handwriting of Dr. James Shirrefs.]

John, son of the said William and Isobel Thain, was married to Mary, daughter of Robert Burnett of Sauchen, and had five children named—

Robert, who died while serving in the Royal Navy.

Jane, who was born the 25th July, 1727, and married to David Shirrefs the 21 Dec., 1748, and died 4th May, 1801.

Andrew, who died in Aberdeen.

John, who died in Jamaica.

Anne, who died in Aberdeen, unmarried, in 1802.

The said David Shirrefs was married to Jane Lunan, the 21st of Dec., 1748, and had children named—

John, born in 1749.—Died in infancy.

James, 1751.

David, 1753.

Mary, 1754.

Burnett, 1756.

Anne, 1758.

Alexander, 1759.

Andrew, 1762.

Thomas, 1763.

Robert, 1765.

Jane, 1770.

James was married (28 Sept., 1790) to Amelia, youngest daughter of James Morison of Elsick, Esq., and had children named—

David, born in 1791.

James, 1793.

Alexander, 1794.

Amelia, 1796.

Jane, 1797.

APPENDIX No. VIII.

KATHERINE SETON FORMAN LEONARD

(Mrs. George Cadenhead).

George Leonard, tailor, burgess of Aberdeen, married Marjorie Fettes, only daughter of William Fettes,
tailor, burgess of Aberdeen, 27th June, 1709.   She
endowed him with her whole estate, which was esti-
mated at one thousand merks.   He bound himself to
"eik and conjune" to the said "dote and tocher" an
equal sum.   Amongst the marriage contract trustees
were a John and a James Leonard.

Of this marriage there were three sons—(1) William,
who married, on 1st March, 1750, Ann, daughter of
John Leonard ; (2) George ; and (3) James.

James (3) married Mary Sampson and had ten
children, whereof nine were alive at 3rd Sept., 1802.
(1) George ; (2) Ann ; (3) Arthur ; (4) John.

Ann (2) married Alexander Kiloh, and had one son,
John Kiloh, bookseller in Aberdeen, and one daughter,
Sarah, now alive (1887).   John Kiloh went to America
and left issue—now numerous in the second, third and
fourth generations.

Arthur (3), merchant-tailor in London, married and
had issue.

John (4), merchant-tailor, London, married, on 16th
July, 1800, Sarah Lyall, his cousin, and died 16th

October, 1848, aged 73. His wife died 17th Dec., 1822, aged 54.

The following is a copy of a record, the greater part of which apparently is in the handwriting of John Leonard :—

1773. James Leonard went to Aberdeen, Aug., 1773.

1774. Mary died the 16th Jany., 1774.

1774. George Leonard of Jamaica died 16 March, 1774.

1774. His mother died 4th March, 1774.

1775. William Leonard sailed for Aberdeen 16th of Septr., 1775.

1774. John died 6th January, 1774.

David died the 9th of August.

1779. James sailed for London the 14th June, 1779.

1780. My apprenticeship with Mr. George Auldjo, Merchant in Aberdeen, commences from this day, being the 1st day of December, 1780, to serve him five years, which ends the 1st December, 1785.

1781. James sailed from London per the Favourite-Gibbons 9th Septr., and arrived the 9th Nov., 1781.

1782. James Leonard died at Aberdeen the 15th February, aged 17 years and four months.

1784. William went to Jamaica December 4.

1785. Nanny sailed from London to Aberdeen July, 1785.

1784. William Leonard sailed for Jamaica Nov. 2.

Nancy Leonard sailed for Scotchland July, 1785.

The last three memos. appear to be in a female hand.

John Leonard and Sarah Lyall had issue (1) James, b. 11 Dec., 1800 ; d. 7 Jan., 1875. (2) George Gordon, b. 11 January, 1803 ; d. 3 Sept., 1803. (3) William, b. 11 December, 1804, m. Blanche Eades; d. 23 April, 1883, *s.p.* (4) Sibella Mary, b. 14 August, 1806 ; m. Dr. James Anderson, H.E.I.C.S. ; d. 17 Jan., 1875, *s.p.* (5) John, b. 18 May, 1808; d. 26 Nov., 1809. (6) Robert Adnam, b. 28 March, 1810 ; d. 23 Jan., 1837.

James Leonard (1), Surgeon in London, spent the earlier part of his professional career in the parish of Strichen, Aberdeenshire ; married, 1st, 9th Sept., 1831, Alice Gray at Aberdeen. She died 6th Dec., 1837. The issue of this marriage were—(1) John William, b. 12 June, 1832 ; m. Fanny Warren, and has issue. (2) Katherine Seaton Forman, b. 21 June, 1834 ; m. George Cadenhead. (3) James Keith, b. 19 Jan., 1836; d. 25 Aug., 1874 ; m. Jean Fortune Blackwell, who survives him, *s.p.* (4) Alice, b. 20 Nov., 1837 ; d. — June, 1839. Married, 2nd, 9th April, 1840, Fanny Whitter, who died 18 Sept., 1849. The issue of this marriage were—(5) Fanny Whitter, b. 27 July, 1841. (6) Alice Elizabeth, b. 12 Feb., 1843 ; m. Thomas Henry Condell and has issue. (7) Jessie, b. 3 August, 1845; m. Robert Mackenzie and has issue. (8) William, b. 12 Dec., 1847 ; m. Catharine Madle and has issue. Dr. James Leonard married, a third time, Amelia Jane Buthlin, widow, and had issue two sons and five daughters.

APPENDIX No. IX.

ALICE GRAY (Mrs. James Leonard).

The tradition of the family obtained from the late
Rev. Dr. Cushny of Rayne, was that they were of the
family of Gray of Schivas. In 1696, when George
Gray was laird of Schivas, Alexander Gray paid poll
tax as tenant of Eastertown of Fyvie.

> Oh I'll get a thiggin frae auld John Black
> An' I'll get anither frae the Lady o' Glack
> An' I'll get a thiggin frae auld Sauners Gray
> For herdin' his yowes sae lang on the brae.
> Quhill o' ye lasses will gae to Balcairn
> Quhill o' ye lasses will gae to Balcairn
> An be the guidwife o' bonny Balcairn.

In 1770 Thomas Gray was tenant of Eastertown of
Fyvie, having four brothers sub-tenants or helpers,
viz., John, afterwards in Broadplace of Daviot ; Adam
in Newtown of Momsie, Daviot ; William in Little
Pitinnan, Daviot ; and Alexander (?)

Thomas Gray removed to Westhall in Oyne, and
rented the home-farm there belonging to General Horn
of Logie-Elphinstone. He was noted for a superior
breed of cattle which he possessed. His ploughs were
drawn, one by ten oxen and two by four horses each.
Possessed of great bodily strength, he was often hurt
in the exercise of it. As a youth he was attending a

train of his father's horses, each carrying on its back
two sacks of grain. Through inattention on the part
of Thomas, who was wondering at the magnificence of
the Gallowgate of Aberdeen, one of the horses collided
on a corner, and its load fell on the street. A neighbouring shopkeeper jeered and said, "I could hae deen
that mysel', Geordie." For answer Thomas lifted the
two sacks together, placed them carefully on the horse's
back, and said, "Could ye hae deen that, man?" About
1766 he married Mary Cuthbert, and died at Westhall
in 1805. He was buried at the "auld kirk of Bethelnie."
The issue of his marriage were (1) Arthur ; (2) Anne
(Mrs. Cushny) ; (3) Sarah (Mrs. Alexander Maitland) ;
(4) Mary (Mrs. Cock); (5) Janet (Mrs. Adam Maitland);
(6) Alexander, Merchant in Aberdeen.

Of Thomas Gray's brothers, John in Broadplace had
two sons, Roderick and Adam, whereof the former
became Provost of Peterhead, was a man of enterprise
and note, and left a considerable fortune.

Adam in Newtown of Momsie had three sons—
Adam, George, and James — and four daughters.
Adam was in Jamaica for forty years, returned and
bought Fingask in Daviot. William in Little Pitinnan
left two sons—William and Alexander—both farmers.
William, a son of one of these, was in Pitinnan in 1872,
having two sons with him, and two in Demarara,
cultivating sugar and coffee.

Arthur (1), eldest son of Thomas Gray, was a Purser
in the Royal Navy. He purchased a small lairdship

in the Garioch. The inscription on his gravestone in the old Kirkyard of Logie is as follows :—

IN MEMORY OF
ARTHUR GRAY, Esq., late of Thripleton,
Who died at Kebbaty
On the 26th July, 1825, aged 57 years ;
Also of
Mrs. JANE MASON, his mother-in-law,
Who died at Harthill on 8th June, 1804,   ·
Aged 70 years ;
And of
MARY MASON, his wife, who died
At Aberdeen, on the 13th day of October,
1843, aged 74 years.

The issue of ARTHUR GRAY and MARY MASON were—

1. Mary, Mrs. Gribble, d. *s.p.* Anne m. Thomas Sangster, Advocate in Aberdeen—had issue, two daughters, Mrs. Roche and Mrs. Skinner, both of whom had issue.

2. Sarah m. Andrew Strachan—had issue William, died young, unmarried. Maria Jane m. 1st Wm. Watson, 2nd James Cock Coutts, and had issue by both marriages.

3. Janet, 1802, m. Dr. John Milne, d. *s.p.*

4. Alice m. James Leonard, and had issue ; d. 6 Dec., 1837.

5. Thomas died young, unmarried.

www.ingramcontent.com/pod-product-compliance
Lightning Source LLC
Chambersburg PA
CBHW030020030726
47499CB00008B/3061